Michael Morpurgo OBE is one of Britain's best writers for children. He has written over 100 books and won many prizes, including the Smarties Prize, the Blue Peter Book Award and the Whitbread Award. His recent bestselling novels include *Shadow, An Elephant in the Garden, Born to Run* and *A Medal for Leroy*.

Michael's stories have been adapted numerous times for stage and screen. *War Horse* is enjoying staggering commercial and critical success as a theatrical production in the West End and on Broadway, and was recently made into a major film by Steven Spielberg. The film based on his novel *Private Peaceful* was also released in October 2012. Michael is a former Children's Laureate and founder, with his wife Clare, of the charity Farms for City Children.

Michael Foreman grew up in a small English fishing village, and has loved the sea ever since. His is one of the most successful and well-loved children's book illustrators of his generation. Among many other honours he has won the Kate Greenaway, the Smarties Prize (both for books which he wrote and illustrated) and the Children's Book Award. His friendship with Michael Morpurgo ("the other Michael") has led to many classic collaborations including *Kaspar, The Amazing Story of Adolphus Tips* and *A Medal for Leroy*.

michael morpurgo

LITTLE MANFRED

ILLUSTRATED BY
MICHAEL FOREMAN

HarperCollins *Children's Books*

First published in hardback in Great Britain
by HarperCollins *Children's Books* 2011

This edition published in Great Britain
by HarperCollins *Children's Books* in 2013

HarperCollins *Children's Books* is a division of HarperCollins*Publishers* Ltd
77-85 Fulham Palace Road, Hammersmith, London W6 8JB

Visit us on the web at www.harpercollins.co.uk

Learn more about Michael Morpurgo and his stories at
www.michaelmorpurgo.com

1

ISBN 978-0-00-749163-6

Printed and bound in England by Clays Ltd, St Ives plc

For Maggie, Jamie, Flora and Isabelle

Contents

Part One   11

Part Two   51

Part Three   87

Part Four   117

Twenty-five years later   137

Afterword   149

Extra Time   163

Part One

THE SEA WAS ten minutes away from the farm, no more. So there was hardly a day of my life that I didn't go down to the beach. It was my favourite place to escape to. Farm chores were definitely not my idea of fun – except bottle-feeding lambs or calves – but if there were sheds to muck out, and there always were, I'd make myself scarce, quick as a twick, and run off down to the beach.

LITTLE MANFRED

The trouble was, that as soon as he was old enough, Alex would always follow me. Alex was my little brother and he talked a lot. He was seven by this time; I was twelve and liked to do my thinking and my sulking on my own. But wherever I went he went, and wherever we went, Mannie came with us – that's Manfred, our black and white sheepdog. We'd go swimming in the sea in summer, all three of us.

We'd chase the gulls whenever we saw them ganging up on the oystercatchers; we'd skim stones if the sea was calm enough – twenty-six bounces was my record – Alex had only ever managed two! Whatever we did, wherever we went, the three of us were always together.

All our friends thought Manfred was a funny sort of a name for a dog. Apparently I'd called him after our toy dog, Little Manfred, a wooden dachshund, painted brown with red wheels. Mum had played with him when she was little. Then I'd had him to play with for a while, and now he belonged to Alex; only Alex wasn't that interested in him any more, mostly because he'd grown out of him, but also because Little Manfred only had three wheels by now, and didn't work very well. Dad had trodden on him the Christmas before, by accident of course. So Little Manfred was 'busted', and Alex never let Dad forget who'd done it. Dad was always saying he'd mend him, but he never did. So there Little Manfred had stood ever since Christmas, lopsided on the sitting-room windowsill, waiting for a new wheel.

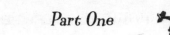

For some reason I never really understood, Little Manfred always seemed more important to Mum than to anyone else. She really cried when the accident happened. I don't think I'd ever seen her so upset. I'd see her looking at Little Manfred so sadly sometimes, stroking his back almost as if he were a real dog. And at Christmas after the accident, she tied a red ribbon round his neck, "to make him feel better," she said.

I didn't discover why she loved him so much or why he was called Little Manfred until one day in that summer of 1966.

I remember the exact day. It was the day after England won the World Cup at Wembley. Both Dad

and Alex were football mad. Just about everyone in England was that summer, except Mum and me. We hated the fuss and ballyhoo, but all the same, I've got to say that I did quite like it when England won. I watched the game on the television with Dad and

Alex. Mum ignored the whole thing, she was just not interested.

Anyway, that next morning I was wandering along the beach with Alex. He had a football at his feet and kept replaying Geoff Hurst's last-minute goal over and over, dribbling the ball down the beach and then letting fly as he scored the goal yet again. Then he was Nobby Stiles, skipping along, holding the cup up high, his socks round his ankles. It made me laugh out loud watching him. And Mannie loved it too, barking his head off and then chasing after the ball wherever Alex kicked it.

It was a wild and blustery day with clouds scudding across the sky. I sat down and watched the

waves tumbling in towards the shore. Mannie was
bored with football by now because Alex kept taking
the ball away from him. Instead he was doing what
he usually did, chasing everything that moved – his

tail first, then gulls, leaves and a paper bag that was

flying low across the beach, just too high for him to

catch. After a while he came running back to me. I

knew what he was after. And I knew too that once I

started the game it would go on for ever. He stood there looking at me adoringly, his eyes pleading with me. I gave in, just as he knew I would. I picked up a stick and threw it into the sea for him. Off he went and back he came, again and again and again.

I had just thrown the stick for the umpteenth time when a pair of oystercatchers flew up suddenly from behind me, out to sea, piping as they went. Something had alarmed them. Mannie was distracted from his game and dropped his stick, which was strange because he was as used to oystercatchers as I was – he didn't usually pay them any attention. His ears were pricked forward, his gaze fixed on something higher up the beach. I thought at first it must be Alex's football. I could see it now. It had landed up there not far from the upturned rowing boat. But it wasn't the football that was bothering him. He had heard something. And I heard it too now, the sound of voices, men's voices. There was a growl in the back of Mannie's throat.

That was when I first saw the two men. They were coming down the track towards the rowing boat at the top of the beach. As they reached it they stood there for some moments, looking out to sea. One of them was carrying a walking stick, and had on a strange hat, with a feather in it; the other was much taller, and was wearing a duffel coat.

They were arm in arm, and leaning into the wind.
Mannie was barking at them by now. I told him to
shut up and, to my surprise, he did exactly as I said.
He came to sit close to me, his head against my leg
for reassurance. Then Alex was beside me too.

"Who are they?" he whispered. The taller of the
two had spotted Alex's football by now and picked
it up.

"Yours?" he called out.

The men looked a little older than Dad. City people, I thought – they had on muddied city shoes, not wellies. Alex nodded and put his finger in his mouth, which he always did when he was nervous.

"I'll bring it down to you," said the man. "Not so good at kicking these days."

Then the one in the hat took the football off him. "*Nein, Nein,* Marty, I shall kick it," he said. "A football should be kicked. It is what a football is for."

He dropped the ball on to the ground, took a step or two back and kicked it. It was a perfectly judged kick, the ball ending up so close to us that Alex had only to bend down to pick it up. The two men laughed, waved at us, and went on their way, down towards the sea, where they stood for a few moments with their backs to us, looking up and down the beach. That was when I heard one of them saying, "It was about here. I think it was about here that it happened. *Ja, Ja*. Here. I am sure."

For a while nothing more was said. Then he went on, "I am so glad that I came back. This was a good idea of yours, Marty. I did not think it was going to be, but it is." He spoke English with a foreign accent of some kind. I could understand him all right, but it wasn't the kind of accent I was used to at all.

"Did I tell you what he was doing, Marty?" the man went on, his voice a little lower. I felt a little guilty eavesdropping like this on their conversation, but I couldn't resist it. I had to go on listening. "He always liked to bounce the stones across the water. He said that this reminded him of his childhood. We were working all morning on the barbed wire that was up there behind us, taking it away, and we were on lunch break. We were all sitting back up at the top of the beach, by the path there, near the boat. There was a boat then too, maybe this one, maybe not. Who knows? He said he had found a nice flat stone and he was going to bounce it across the sea, all the way to Germany. And then he walked away from us down to the water to where we are standing now, maybe a little further out because it was low tide that day."

I was close enough to hear that the words were catching in his throat, that he was struggling to control his voice.

"You know what you should do, Walter?" said his friend, and he bent down and picked up a pebble. "Here, this is a good one. Why don't you throw one for him, right now, all the way to Germany, just like he did?"

Even as he was throwing the stone I knew exactly what Mannie would do, but I was too slow to stop him. Mannie was after it in a flash. He was already plunging into the shallows before the pebble landed in the sea. I was yelling at him to stop, "Mannie! Mannie! Manfred! Come back!"

But no amount of shouting would be any use – I knew that. He would come back when he felt like it and not before. The two men had turned, and were coming up the beach towards us now, the one in the hat waving his stick at us. As they came closer I could see that both of them were frowning. They weren't angry frowns exactly, but it was obvious they weren't at all pleased with us. I felt Alex's hand steal into mine as they came nearer.

"I'm sorry," I said, "but if you throw something, Mannie goes after it. He's like that. He can't help himself."

Then Mannie made it worse. He came bounding up to them, shaking himself all over them, and then

sat down in frantic anticipation at their feet, tongue hanging out, longing for another stick or stone to be thrown.

"You called this dog Manfred?" said the man

in the hat, the one with the strange accent. The feather in his hat, I noticed then, was green, just like the hat.

"Yes," I told him. "Manfred or Mannie – we call him both – Manfred when I'm cross with him. He's a farm dog really. He rounds up the sheep and the cows for Dad. But he chases anything. Like I said, he can't seem to stop himself."

The man was shaking his head in disbelief. "Marty, did you hear that?" he said. "This is *wundebar.* It was the name of the dog, the name she chose for him herself! You remember? I told you." Then he turned to us again. "And so you live also on a farm? I must know where it is, this farm."

Alex suddenly found his voice and his courage,

and spoke up. "Course we live on a farm, else we wouldn't have sheep and cows, would we?"

It sounded a bit cheeky so I squeezed Alex's hand to shut him up. I wasn't at all sure I should say where we lived – after all they were both complete strangers to us then. I thought about it. There was nothing threatening about them, and from the look on their faces, I could tell that this was something they really wanted to know, that it was important to them. That's why I told them, I suppose. "It's on the edge of the village," I said, "behind the school and the church. About a mile away. Not far."

"I thought so. I thought so," said the man. "It is near the church, in Kessingland, *nicht wahr*?"

he asked me. His eyes were bright with excitement now. "And the farm you live on, it is called Mayfield Farm, perhaps?"

"How do you know that, Mister?" Alex asked him, rather bluntly. "We haven't never even seen you before."

"No, young man," he replied with a smile. "I have not seen you before, but if I am not mistaken, I have been to your farm. I think I know every ditch on this farm, every hedge, every barn." He turned to his friend. "This is wonderful, Marty, *ausgezeichnet*." Then back to me again. "And I think maybe your mother, she is called Grace, *ja*? Am I right?"

I couldn't believe it. The man seemed to know so much about us – our home, even our mum's name – and I hadn't told him anything. As he turned away from us I could see he was near to tears. He walked away on his own up to the top of the beach, where he sat down by the upturned rowing boat.

That was when his friend spoke up. "I think

Walter needs a little time on his own," he said – he spoke English a bit more like we did. "This was always going to be a difficult day for him. Coming back, it is never easy, you know."

I hadn't a clue what he was talking about, and I think it must have showed, because, without my even asking, he went on to explain.

"Well," he said. "This is going to be difficult for you to believe, but it looks to me as if my friend Walter over there must have known your mother a long time ago when she was a girl. All he has told me, all I know for sure – and he hasn't told me much – is that a long, long time ago, just after the war, Walter lived for a while on a farm round here,

near Kessingland. And it's looking to me now, and

to him I think, very much as if it might have been

on your farm. He lived there for nearly two years,

I believe. And he did say something about a dog

there called Little Manfred and a girl called Grace. So when he comes here to this beach – which he clearly remembers so well – and he meets a dog called Manfred, and then he discovers you very probably live in the actual farmhouse where he lived, and that your mother is called Grace – well, you can imagine, it must have come as quite a shock to him. A nice shock, but a shock all the same. We'll go and see how he is, shall we?"

As we walked together up the beach, he introduced himself to us as Mr Soper. Then he added, "Marty. You can call me Marty, if you like. I don't even know your names, do I?"

"She's Charley," said Alex, seemingly quite

happy now to chat away, "which is a boy's name, but she's a girl. She's my sister, and I'm Alex and I'm seven and a quarter. That man by the boat, who speaks funny, who is he?"

"Walter?" Marty replied. "Walter is a very old friend of mine from Germany. He came over to England to go to Wembley for the World Cup Final – he's a big football fan, like me. But also he came to see me, and I thought it would be a grand idea to come here to see if he could find the place again, the farm where he stayed at the end of the war. It's the first time he's been back in England since he left, and that was nearly twenty years ago."

"Wowee!" said Alex, beside himself, as I knew

he would be, with excitement – about Wembley, about the football match. "You were really there? At the match? At Wembley? Wowee!"

Marty nodded. "I was," he replied with a smile. "We both were, Walter and me. So I came away happy. But he was not so happy – which is quite understandable when you think about it."

"You were at the match yesterday? You actually saw it?" Alex still couldn't believe it. "That goal of ours," he went on, "it did go over the line, didn't it? The ref was right, wasn't he?"

I was fed up with this. "It's just a game, a silly game," I said. Dad and Alex had gone on and on about that stupid goal.

"Football not your thing then?" Marty asked me. I shrugged.

Still Alex wouldn't leave it alone. "Well, did it go over the line or didn't it? You were there. You must have seen."

"Who knows?" Marty replied. "Walter and me, we talked about little else all the way here in the car. Funnily enough, *he* thought it wasn't over the line and *I* thought it was – not that we're biased, either of us, of course. But in the end, it doesn't matter, does it? It was a great game. And like you said,

Charley, when all's said and done, I suppose, it was just a game. Someone had to win, someone had to lose. We got lucky yesterday, that's all. It's like Walter meeting up with you today on this beach. He got lucky. I'm sure he's forgotten all about the match. Coming here, meeting you, being in touch with his memories – I can tell you, this means a whole lot more to him than any football match, win or lose – even the World Cup."

Walter was still sitting down beside the upturned boat at the top of the beach. He was lost in his thoughts until he heard us coming and looked up. Mannie was running on ahead now, a cuttlefish in his mouth. He dropped it at Walter's

feet and sat down, tongue hanging, tail wagging
across the pebbles, waiting for it to be thrown.
Walter reached out to fondle his ears. "Manfred,"

he murmured, "Little Manfred." Then he asked me,

"Do you know why this dog is called Manfred?"

"Sort of," I said. "It was because Mum had a

toy dog, a wooden one, called Little Manfred, and then I played with him when I was little."

"And then me," Alex piped up. "He was mine, and then Dad trod on him at Christmas and the wheel got busted and so now he doesn't work. He just falls over all the time."

"Anyway," I said, trying to shut Alex up, who was always interrupting, "when I was little we got this new sheepdog puppy and I called him Manfred, after Little Manfred because he was my favourite toy, and everyone thought that was a good name. So it sort of stuck."

"But we call him Mannie mostly," Alex added, "not Manfred."

"Ah, yes," Walter went on, "but do you know why this toy dog of yours was called Little Manfred in the first place?" He took off his feathered hat and tried to smooth down his hair, but it was blowing everywhere and he couldn't make it lie down. It was silver-white and wispy. He looked suddenly older without his hat. "I think you should sit down out of the wind. You will be cold. This will take a little while."

Part Two

WALTER HANDED HIS hat to Alex to hold, and I could see that Alex liked that – he seemed fascinated by the feather. It was some time before Walter spoke again.

"Manfred, me and the others, we used to sit right here in this place and have our lunch," Walter began, "right by this boat. I think it was the same boat. It is older now, like me." He was looking out to sea as he spoke, deep in his thoughts, lost in his memories.

"We used to try to look over the horizon, I remember. We used to make a joke that if we looked hard enough we might be able to see Germany and home. Bavaria – I came from Bavaria, and so did Manfred. Bavaria is a long way from the sea, of course. But Manfred and me, we always felt we were closer to home here on the beach than anywhere else."

It seemed to me almost as if he were talking to himself, that he was just letting his thoughts find the words they needed.

"Manfred lived in my street, in my town, Regensburg. We went to the same school, played football in the same team. You could say we grew up like twin brothers who became best friends. When he got married to Jutta, I was his best man. And when little Inga was born, I was made her godfather. We joined the navy on the very same day.

This was only a few months before the war began.

"All the way through our training in the Kriegsmarine, the German navy, Manfred was at my side. And then we found ourselves serving on the same ship. The *Bismarck*. We could not have been more proud. We knew this was the finest battleship in the German navy, the fastest in the world, thirty knots, 50,000 tons. Every sailor in the Fatherland wanted to serve on her. It was a great honour and privilege to be chosen to sail in this ship."

To start with I worried that Alex would interrupt him to ask some stupid question or other, but then I realised that he was completely absorbed.

Part Two

Alex sat there cross-legged, unable to take his eyes off Walter's face. I very soon found I was lost in his story myself.

"There were over 2,000 men on board," Walter went on, "and every one of us believed that nothing in the world could beat us. We were young and full of – the word is *bravado*, I think. Everyone was like this in those early days of the war. Our commander, Captain Lindemann, promised us victory. Of course, we believed him; we believed everything we were told. We were sure that if any ship of the Royal Navy dared to come within range of our guns we could blow it out of the water. So when we steamed out of Gotenhafen that day – this was in the spring

of 1941 – we had no doubt in our hearts, only pride,
a fierce and foolish pride. When we went into our
first battle in the Denmark Strait, we were quite
sure of victory.

"The captain told us afterwards, Manfred and
me and the others on the gun crew, that it was a
shell from our gun that destroyed the *Hood*. The
Hood was the pride of the Royal Navy, the biggest

battleship they had. It was something we could not believe when we saw it. She just blew up and sank within a few minutes. There were some who cheered – many, I am ashamed to say. But Manfred and me, we both knew there was nothing to cheer about, that in those few short moments, as we looked on, hundreds and hundreds of sailors had died. They were seamen like us, fighting for their country like us. I think this was the first time I began to understand that this is what happens in war. You kill people. People kill you."

He found it difficult to go on, and had to take a deep breath before he did. It was as if he was telling the story of a nightmare he could not forget.

Part Two

"The other British ships made smoke and turned away. Our first battle was over and we had won a famous victory. It was just as we had been told: *Bismarck* was the most powerful battleship in the world. All over the ship we knew we had beaten the best the Royal Navy could send against us, so of course we were even more sure that nothing could stop us now. Everyone on the ship was happy, and I knew I should be happy with them. But I was not. At night when I closed my eyes, I could see the *Hood* blowing up, and I could not sleep. I heard the cries of drowning sailors. I thought I would never sleep again.

"For a few days after this, it was as if the

Part Two

Bismarck ruled the seas. With *Prinz Eugen*, another of our most powerful ships, we steamed out into the Atlantic. The ocean was ours. The world was ours. We could sink any ship we found. Of course, we knew the British would come after us, that there would be more battles ahead. We did not 'give a monkey's' as you say, I think – I like this expression. And by now we believed we were invincible.

"Even when the torpedo from the bomber plane hit our rudder, and we knew we could no longer manoeuvre properly, even when the British fleet was closing in all around us, still we believed that we would fight them off and reach the safety of a French port, that we would be able to make

our repairs and come out again to finish what we started. We believed this maybe because we wanted to believe it. Even when we were being bombarded from all sides and the ship was not able to move any more and all our guns were out of action, I never thought we would sink. I promise you: even when we heard the order to Abandon Ship, we could not imagine the *Bismarck* was going down. It just was not possible.

"It was only in the cold of the water, with the sea on fire, with men screaming and dying all around me, that at last I had to accept the truth of what was happening. My leg was damaged, broken – I do not know how, but I found I could not use it. Manfred had hold of me and was swimming me away when

we saw the *Bismarck* disappear beneath the waves.

There was a terrible groaning as

she went down and – a sound I

shall never forget – a

long sigh of steam and smoke as if the ship was breathing her last breath. All around us there were drowning sailors. It was like the sinking of the *Hood* all over again, only this time it was me that was going to die, Manfred too, all of us.

"I am not a brave man – I know this now – but I was not frightened. I think perhaps I just knew that there was nothing more I could do. I remember thinking that dying must always be like this, that to make it easy you have only to give in to it. I know that without Manfred I would have given up and let myself drown. I was too weak, too cold to go on struggling. I had lost my will to survive. But Manfred held me up, kept talking to me, telling me that help was coming, that we would be all right.

"I do not know how long we were in the water – Manfred said I was only half conscious most of the time. All I know is that when I looked up I saw the side of a great ship, close to us, so close I could almost reach out and touch it. With Manfred's help, I grabbed the scramble net and held on. How Manfred got me up that net I do not know. He must have dragged me up. My leg of course was useless, so I could not have done it on my own. Then I was being pulled on to the deck. I was more dead than alive, I think. When I opened my eyes I saw the face of this man." He was pointing at Marty, smiling through his tears. "This same man, who is sitting right beside you now. Marty."

Marty reached out and patted his arm. "Excuse me, Walter, it was Able Seaman, First Class, Martin Soper of *HMS Dorsetshire*, if you please." Then Marty turned to us and took up the story himself.

"I'm telling you, when I first saw Walter lying there on the deck of our ship, he was like a fish out of water, gasping for breath. He was coughing up seawater, half the Atlantic. And he was covered, head to toe, in black oil. His friend, Manfred, was too. There were hundreds and hundreds of them still in the sea, dozens of them struggling up the nets. Manfred spoke a little English; you spoke none,

Walter, not then. Manfred told me you had a broken leg, probably, and I remember I called the doc over to have a look. He said to get you on a stretcher and take you below to the sickbay, to get you cleaned up and warm, that he'd be down to look after you as soon as he could, but that there were hundreds of urgent cases to see to first on deck, and so he might be some time.

"Manfred and me, we were just getting Walter on to the stretcher when we felt the ship beginning to move under us. We knew well enough it wasn't just the swell of the sea or the wind because we could hear the engines roaring. Everywhere – on deck, on the scramble nets, in the sea all around – people were shouting and screaming. Then we heard the Captain's voice coming over the intercom, telling us there were reports of U-boats in the area, that we had to get under way at once, that we had no choice. Stay where we were, the Captain said, and we would be a sitting duck, an easy target for torpedoes.

"The ship was already turning and steaming away. We had to stand there and watch. We left nearly 2,000 men to drown, not the enemy to us any more, who had sunk the *Hood*, but fellow sailors. For one sailor to leave another sailor to drown, no matter what uniform he wears, cries out against all he believes in, against all the traditions of the sea. To leave one would be bad enough. To leave 2,000… I still see those men in the water every day of my life."

"But you did pick up nearly a hundred of us,

Marty," said Walter. "I have told you often that you must never forget this. On the *Hood*, they never got a chance – only three of them survived."

For a while, neither one of them spoke, but looked out to sea, each lost in his own thoughts. The silence was broken by a pair of gulls, screeching and swooping overhead.

I said the first thing that came into my head. "My dad says that every gull you hear is the ghost of a dead sailor, letting you know he's still alive."

"I don't believe in ghosts," Alex said, turning on me, "and you know I hate it when you talk about them."

"I also do not believe in ghosts," Walter told him, "but I do like this idea of your father's very much. If I must be a bird in my next life, I wish to be a gannet, not a gull. I want to be able to dive like a gannet, and I shall float high on the air as they do. Up there they are free. They love their freedom, I think. To be free, this is the most important thing of all, for birds, for people too."

He picked up a handful of pebbles and scattered them out on to the beach, like dice. It was as if he was speaking out his thoughts in much the same way.

"We saw many gannets, I remember," he said, "on the day I came to England on *HMS Dorsetshire*.

I was now a prisoner of war, of course. When I
looked up at the gulls crying in the sky back then, I
thought, *They are free up there; I am not. What are
they crying for*? I could not know it then, and nor
did Manfred, of course, but we would be prisoners

of war for six long years."

"Six years?" I said. "That's like for ever."

"You are right," he went on. "But I had Manfred with me. Without him… well, it would have been much harder for me. We were lined up on the quayside, all of us, all the survivors of the *Bismarck*, and Marty came over to us to say goodbye. You remember this, Marty? None of the other British sailors did this. Only you. You shook us by the hand, Manfred and me, and you gave us cigarettes too. I never forgot this kindness, nor did Manfred. They took us away up to the north of England to a prisoner-of-war camp and after that I did not see you again, Marty, did I? Not for a long, long time.

"I will be honest with you. At first, Manfred and I, we could not forgive the British navy for what they did when they left our comrades to drown in

the sea. For a long time we were angry. But the
more we talked about it and thought about it during
our years as prisoners of war, the more we came

Part Two

to understand that the British had good reason not to forgive us also. Those 2,000 men on the *Hood* who had died had families too. How could they ever forgive the gun crew who did what we had done? We thought much about this, Manfred and me, and we talked about it often, quietly, between ourselves. It is never out of my mind even now.

"When I learned later on what had happened to so many of my friends, from the navy, from school, from my home town, I think after all I was lucky to be safe in my prison camp in England. It was cold in the winters and the food was never enough. But we had Red Cross parcels and letters from home. They made us work hard in the fields, picking up stones, spreading manure, making roads. But no one was shooting at us, no one was bombing us. The war seemed far away. So it was not so bad for us.

"I think perhaps Manfred found it harder than I did being a prisoner. It took weeks, sometimes months for a letter to arrive from Jutta, and he longed to see Inga, his little daughter, again. He had only seen her for such a short time, just for one week when he was home on leave, before we sailed on the *Bismarck*. They came to wave us off, I remember. We both lived on our memories, I think, but as time went by I would often see Manfred standing there looking out through the wire and

I knew what he was dreaming of. I could see the sadness in his eyes and I could tell he was finding it harder and harder to be without Jutta and Inga.

"As for me, like Manfred, like the rest of the men in the camp, I longed only for the end of the war, to be a free man again. So when it came at last, in the summer of 1945, we were just happy it was all over and we would be going home.

"But sadly this did not happen, not for a long time. They would not let us go home. Instead we were moved down to a prisoner-of-war camp near here in Suffolk, to work on the farms and sometimes to clear the beaches of wire and mines. And this was how, in the end, Manfred and I were let out of the camp and came to be housed with a family in Mayfield Farm, and so

Part Two

we found ourselves living there with a farmer and his wife, Mr and Mrs Williams." He paused then, and smiled at us. "And their daughter, a little girl called Grace."

Part Three

ALEX, I could tell, was still trying to work it out. "So was that our mum, Charley?" he whispered to me. But Alex could never whisper softly.

Walter answered him for me. "I think so. I am very much hoping so. Maybe you understand now why I am so happy to have met you like this, and all by chance, by accident. It is as if it was meant to be."

But there was something that was still bothering me. "I still don't understand why your friend, Manfred, has the same name as our dog," I said.

"Ah yes, Little Manfred," Walter went on. "Do not worry, I have not forgotten Little Manfred. He is not a dog I could ever forget, I promise you. I will tell you about him soon enough. But let me tell you first about Mr and Mrs Williams – this is your grandmother and your grandfather, I think. As I told you, it was their farmhouse we were staying in, Manfred and I.

"To start with, I must say, they were just polite, but not at all friendly. I do not think they wanted us there at all. They did not like having to lodge us in the house – we were Germans after all. The war was over, but we were still the enemy. And little Grace, she would not even be polite. She did not speak to us for weeks; sometimes she used to stick her tongue out at us, I remember. But Manfred, he managed in the end to make friends with her. He talked to her a lot about Inga, showed Grace her photograph. He built her a tree house in the garden, where she could sit and read. She loved to read books."

"She still does," Alex said. "Mum's always reading. We watch telly, she reads books. I don't like books. They've got spellings in them." I shushed Alex, and Walter went on.

"But it wasn't long before they were treating us as if we were a part of the family. They let us eat with them at their table; we even went to church with them on Sundays. We worked with them, looking after the horses, ploughing, harvesting, spreading muck on the fields, fetching water, digging ditches, picking stones off the fields, whatever it was that needed doing. I was always a little slower than the others, because I had to walk with a stick, after my injury. But I was a hard worker. And on the days we were not needed on the farm, we were sent to work with the other prisoners down on the beaches, clearing the wire and the mines. There were mines all round the coast, you see. They had been put there, years before, to stop an invasion from the sea. But of course in the end there never was an invasion. Then after the war was over, we prisoners of war, we had to help clear it all away, to make the beaches safe again.

"In the evenings, Manfred would often sit and read a story to Grace – I remember this very well. I did it sometimes myself, if Manfred was still out feeding the animals after dark. But I knew always that Grace liked it better when Manfred was there. His English was much better than mine, although after two years living there, I could speak it quite well.

"At Christmas, Manfred and I sang to them some German carols – that was Mrs Williams's idea. Manfred taught Grace to sing '*Stille Nacht*', '*Silent Night*', in German. And, in the end, the villagers were kind – for most of the time, anyway. There were one or two who crossed the street to the

other side, so they did not have to speak to us, but

we had to expect that. In this war many had suffered

greatly, had great griefs and sadnesses to bear; and

where there is sadness, there is often anger. I think

perhaps that the anger lasts longer even than the sadness. For Manfred, Grace became almost like a daughter, the daughter he was parted from. I never saw him happier than when he was with her.

"Then at last came the good news that Manfred and I were soon to be going home. This was when Manfred decided he would make something special for Grace, a gift from us both to leave behind. Manfred loved to make things, out of wood usually. He had always been clever with his hands. Anyway, he found some bits of wood in the barn – this wood, I remember, came from apple crates in the barn – and out of this wood he carved a little dog, a dachshund like the one he and Jutta and

little Inga had at home. He made wheels for it too.
I painted it – a brown body, of course, with a little
black nose, eyes, ears, and a green chassis too. And
the wheels, I painted bright red."

"Little Manfred!" said Alex. "You painted
Little Manfred?"

"Manfred made him, and I painted him," Walter told him proudly. "We made Little Manfred together. I tied on a piece of string too, so Grace could pull him along. This was all done in secret, in the bedroom we shared together, because we wanted it to be a surprise for her. Manfred said it would be like a 'dog of peace'. I have always remembered those words. We were very pleased with him, and hid him away under my bed so that we could give him to Grace on the day we left.

"We spent the last day down on the beach, clearing more of the barbed wire – there was always more. When we were having our lunch, Manfred and me and the others, we came up here to sit by

this boat. We were looking out to sea just like I am
doing now. Then Manfred showed me a flat stone
he had found. He told me that he would bounce it
all the way to Germany. It would get back home
before we did, he said. So he got up and went down
to the sea to throw his stone. The tide was far out
that day, I remember, so he had a long walk.

"There was suddenly a great flash and I was
thrown up against the side of the boat by the force
of the explosion. I hit my head, and I think I was
unconscious for some time. How long I lay there,

I do not know. When I woke up they told me what

had happened. It was a mine that blew Manfred up,

one that had not been discovered. They told me that

they were very sorry. This is why I was alone that

evening when I gave Grace the little dog Manfred had made. She was so upset she could not speak. But later, after Grace had gone up to bed, Mrs Williams told me that Grace had decided to call the dog 'Little Manfred', and that she would keep it for ever, that they would all think of Manfred every time they looked at this little dog, and remember how good he was, and kind.

"The lorry came to take me away the next morning. Grace was there in her dressing gown to say goodbye, clutching Little Manfred to her. This was the last time I saw your mother."

He paused then and I thought that was the end of his story.

"Mum always said that Little Manfred was very special to her, her favourite toy," I told him, "that I had to look after him, but she never told me why. And she was really upset too, when Dad trod on him and broke the wheel; not angry, just upset. She was crying, and I didn't know why. I do now."

"But still you do not know everything, not quite," Walter went on. "I should not be here today without my good friend Marty. It was his idea, coming back here, this whole trip. He said it would be good for me, good for both of us, and I think he was right. What was it you said, Marty? 'You have to face the past if you are going to understand it', something like that, wasn't it?' And now here I am, back on this beach where it all happened. It is a place I have dreamed of so often, and of the farm too, and Grace and Manfred."

Alex was up on his feet suddenly, his football

in his hands. "I've got the bestest idea. You've got to come home and see Mum and Dad, and then you can see Little Manfred again too, can't you?"

Walter looked at me. "I am not sure," he said. "Your mother, she might not recognise me. It is a very long time since she has seen me – nearly twenty years!"

"I think Walter is right," said Marty. "We can't just drop in uninvited."

"You are invited," Alex insisted. He wasn't taking no for an answer. "I invited you, didn't I? Come on!" And he was pulling Walter to his feet.

The two men did not know that once Alex got an idea he wanted to do something, then he just went

ahead and did it. So that's how we found ourselves following Alex up the path from the beach. He dribbled the ball all the way, scoring goal after goal through every open gateway we passed, Mannie chasing after every one – twelve of them

before we got home.

"Twelve-nil! Twelve-nil to England!" Alex shouted as we came into the farmyard, and then he did his Nobby Stiles act all over again, skipping and larking about, and that's why he tripped over in the

didn't say so. It didn't bother him though. He just picked himself up and raced on ahead of us towards the house, shouting for Mum to come out. Moments later she appeared at the door, a lamb under one arm, and a feeding bottle in her other hand.

"What is it?" she said. At first I wondered why she wasn't having a go at Alex about his filthy hands and filthy trousers. But she hadn't even seen him. She was standing there stock still, gazing at Walter. For a few moments she and Walter simply stared at one another, and said nothing.

Then Walter said, "Grace? It is me. Walter. You remember?"

"I know it's you," she told him. "I'm just trying

to believe it, that's all." She was rooted to the spot.

I could almost see her thinking about what she

should do. When she made up her mind at last,

she came walking towards us across the farmyard. Walter was holding out his hand to her, but instead of taking it, she handed me the lamb, and gave Alex the bottle to hold. Then she turned to Walter and threw her arms round him, and hugged him, eyes tight shut, but they couldn't hold in the tears.

That was when Dad came out into the yard from the calf shed. Alex ran over to him, holding up his mucky hands and showing them off. "Mum's crying," he said. "And I fell over, Dad. Look!"

Part Four

AN HOUR OR SO later, we were all sitting round the kitchen table – Alex and me, Mum and Dad, Walter and Marty – with Little Manfred on his three wheels, centre stage on the table now, and Mannie curled up in his basket in the corner of the room, keeping an eye on us all.

There were scones and jam out on the table and Battenburg cake. Alex had hardly stopped talking since we got back home. He was telling them Walter's whole story, in his own gabbling and garbled way: how we had met up on the beach, and particularly about Walter and Marty going to the World Cup Final, all about the battleships that had

sunk in the war, how Walter had been a prisoner of war, and how his friend Manfred had been killed down on the beach, and how he was the one who had made Little Manfred. I could hardly get a word in edgeways, and neither could anyone else, until the moment came when his mouth was so full of cake that he had no choice but to stop talking.

"Isn't it supreme?" I said to Mum. "How we met them there by accident, and if we hadn't found them then, you wouldn't ever have met Walter again and we wouldn't be all having tea together? I mean, how amazing is that?"

No one seemed to know quite what to say. Even Alex was silent. For a while there was only the tinkling of teaspoons on teacups. Mum offered Walter more tea. She'd hardly said a word since they had met out in the farmyard. I think she was still trying to take it all in. Then she said, "I remember so well that last time you were sitting here, Walter, when you gave me Little Manfred. He was on the table, just as he is now. It was the evening before you left, I think, the same day Manfred was killed, wasn't it?"

Although she was trying to smile, I could see there were still tears in her eyes, and in her voice too. Dad must have noticed this as well, because he changed the subject fast.

"What d'you think of the match, then?" he asked Marty. "Was that a goal or wasn't it?"

"Oh, for goodness' sake, Harry," Mum said, pulling herself together again and blowing her nose. "What does a stupid goal matter? This is what matters: Walter being here, us being together after all these years, and with Little Manfred too, even though, thanks to you, he's only got three wheels on him."

"You keep saying you're going to mend him, Dad," said Alex, "and you never do. And you're the one who busted him in the first place."

Dad was making his usual excuses about things being a bit busy out on the farm, how he'd get round to it as soon as he could. That was when Marty spoke up. "I have an idea," he said. He turned to Mum. "Maybe I could mend it. Grace, do you have a sewing box by any chance?"

"Of course," she said.

"You can't sew on a wheel," Alex scoffed.

"Well, I think maybe I can," Marty said, "in a sort of way. You'll see. I'll do it after tea."

Then I asked Mum something that had been

on my mind ever since I'd heard Walter's story. "How come you didn't tell me before about Little Manfred, or Manfred, or about Walter? You never said anything."

She thought a while before she spoke. "I suppose because it was so sad, Charley," she said. "When you were very little, I thought it was just too painful to tell you. And then later, well, it was always too awful for me even to think about, let alone talk about. Manfred was such a gentle man, so kind to me. But now Walter is here, maybe all that sadness is over and done with."

"There's one thing I still don't get about all this," Dad said, helping himself to another piece of Battenburg cake. "How did you two find one another again after the war was over?"

"Luck, sheer fluke, wasn't it, Walter?" Marty told him. "I was at Liverpool Street Station only a couple of years after the war ended – 1947 it must have been, I think – out of the navy by this time, and back in civvie street. I was on my way to work in the office – I was in the insurance business in those days, in the City. And there were these men standing together in a huddle on the platform, waiting for a train by the looks of them. I knew at once they were German prisoners of war – they were wearing their navy-blue battle dress. One of them was sitting on a suitcase and he was looking

right at me, frowning at me he was, and staring, as if he knew me. I recognised him at once. It was Walter.

"We hardly had a moment to talk, but it was long enough for us to shake hands and exchange addresses. It was all we had time for, wasn't it, Walter? Then you went off on your train back home to Germany and I went to the office."

"I remember that you gave me a packet of cigarettes again too!" Walter said, "And ever since that meeting we have been writing to one another, every couple of months. These letters were very important to me. Coming home after the war, after so long away, it was not so easy. I think I was like a different person. I was a stranger to my family. It was Jutta and Inga, Manfred's family, who saved me. In time, my friendship for Jutta turned into love, and we were married together a couple of years after I got home. It seemed the most natural thing to do,

not to take Manfred's place, no one could do that.
But to be with her, it felt right for us. And now my
goddaughter was my stepdaughter.

"But even with this new family I found there
were many things I could not talk about. I could
write about them in my letters to Marty. It is difficult

to understand, but even in the short time Marty and I were together on board *HMS Dorsetshire*, seeing what we had on that terrible day, there was a kind of bond between us, I think. Maybe it is because both of us had our nightmares – the sinking of those ships, the *Hood* and the *Bismarck*, the horror of it all, the loss of friends. No one else at home was interested in all this. Why should they be? They wanted only to find enough food, to keep warm, to build their lives again. For them it was a war they just wanted to forget. For us it was still a war we needed to understand.

"So over the years, we became friends through our letters, didn't we, Marty? And the more we wrote to each other, the more we found there was much we had in common. We both of us liked fishing, and football – different teams, of course: Manchester United and Bayern Munich. And then, less than a week or two ago, comes – 'out of the blue', as you say it – the invitation from Marty to come to England. He has two tickets for the World Cup Final, England against Germany. We must go there together, he said. Jutta said I should go. Inga said I should go. And what Inga says I do!

"So I came, and here I am. It is true, we lost the game in the end. But I tell myself, it is only a game, that next time we will win, maybe. I want to tell you that when I look round this table I know that coming back here – to our English family, Manfred's and mine – was better than any match could ever be, even if we had won it. Like you say, Grace, this is more important, much more important.

"When Marty said I should come here to Suffolk, he said it would help to *lay the ghost*. You were right. Manfred would be so pleased to see us here, all of us together, with Little Manfred on his three wheels. Looking at him now, he is just what Manfred said he was, I think, 'a dog of peace'. At last, I can feel that it really is all over now."

"Which reminds me," said Marty, turning to Mum. "He needs a new wheel, doesn't he? I'll need that sewing box of yours, Grace. Do you mind?" He reached out and picked up Little Manfred. "We'll soon fix you up," he said, and then he disappeared with Mum into the sitting room.

There was a lot of whispering going on in there, and the little tap-tapping of a hammer too. Only a few minutes later, Mum came back in, holding Little Manfred triumphantly in both hands. He had four wheels – well, sort of.

"Little Manfred is all mended," she said, beaming at us. She put him down in the centre of the table again. One wheel was a cotton reel and looked just about the same size as the others, only it wasn't red. Alex sorted that out later, crayoning

the new wheel a bright crimson. But best of all,
when he pulled up the string and ran with it, Little
Manfred didn't fall over. He didn't even wobble.
His new wheel worked a treat.

And that was it. That's how I found out why
Little Manfred was called Little Manfred.

But – though I didn't know it then – that wasn't
the end of the story, not quite.

Twenty-five years later

TWENTY-FIVE YEARS LATER I went off on a very special trip to London. Lots of people travelled down from Suffolk with us, a full coachload from the village, including my whole family, Mum, Dad, my own children too, all four of them. My brother Alex even came over from Canada, from Toronto,

where he lives now. But sadly, not everyone could be there. Walter had died the year before. Jutta was there, though, and so was Inga. They came over from Germany especially for the event, and brought

lots of friends and family with them. Marty was
there too, old and frail now, walking stiffly and
slowly, but he said he wouldn't have missed this
for the world. I had to point out to him rather

apologetically, that his cotton-reel wheel had been replaced, so that all four wheels were identical now.

"If you ask me, I think he looks much happier with four good legs," he said, smiling. "Legs, wheels, cotton reels – what's the difference, so long as they work, so long as you can get along. When you get old, that's important."

Inga was the one who got to carry Little Manfred up the steps into the Imperial War Museum, and Mum helped her to set him down in his new home, a display case right in the centre of the great hall where everyone could see him. There was a short welcoming ceremony to mark the occasion, and a speech or two.

We were all standing around afterwards, some of us still a bit tearful, when I noticed a mother and daughter crouching down beside the display case. Both were peering in at Little Manfred.

"What's that sausage dog doing there?" the girl asked.

Her mother was reading the caption beside the showcase, and doing her best to explain. "It says here," she began, "that the dog is called Little Manfred. He was made by two German prisoners

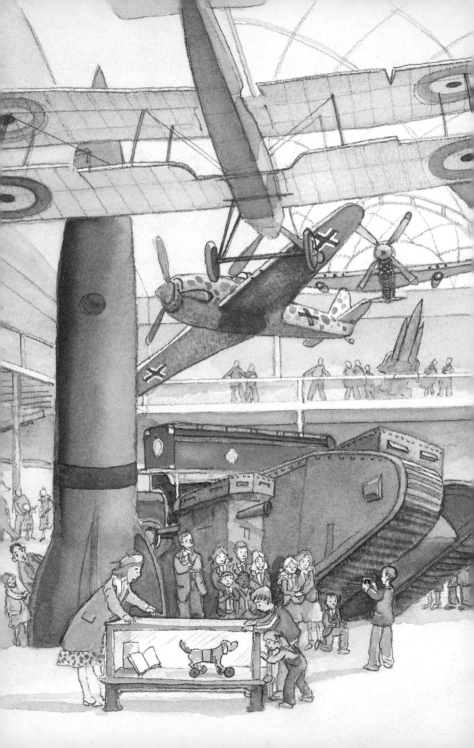

of war, Manfred Heide and Walter Kreuz, when they were staying on a farm in Suffolk after the war. They were working on the farm and helping to clear nearby beaches of barbed wire and mines. It has been given to the museum in their memory."

"But why did they make it? Who was it for?" the little girl asked.

"I don't know," said her mother, "but it says that someone's written a book about it, with pictures. It's called *Little Manfred*. Maybe we can go and find it in the bookshop. We could read it, couldn't we? Then we'll know the whole story, won't we?"

As they walked away, the little girl was looking back over her shoulder. "That little dog, I think he's smiling at me," she said.

Afterword

THE GERMAN BATTLESHIP *BISMARCK* was named after the nineteenth century statesman Otto von Bismarck, first chancellor of the newly unified German Empire. *Bismarck* was launched on 14th February 1939. At the time, she was the largest battleship afloat – more than 50,000 tonnes when fully loaded – and the pride of the German fleet.

On 19th May 1941, under the command of Captain Ernst Lindemann, and with a crew of 2,200 men, *Bismarck* set out from a port in the

Baltic into the North Atlantic. She was accompanied by the heavy cruiser *Prinz Eugen*, on a mission to intercept and destroy Allied merchant shipping. The British Home Fleet were alerted and on the evening of 23rd May, the cruiser HMS *Norfolk* spotted the two German ships on course for the Denmark Strait between Greenland and Iceland. Britain's newest battleship HMS *Prince of Wales* and the older battle-cruiser HMS *Hood* altered their course in order to intercept her. In a brief action the next day, *Hood* was blown up and sunk. Out of her crew of 1,418, only three men survived. In response, there was a determined effort to pursue and destroy *Bismarck*, who had also been hit but managed to get away, making for a port in German-occupied France for repairs.

For a time, contact was lost between *Bismarck* and her pursuers, but on 26th May she was sighted again. A torpedo strike was launched against her by Swordfish aircraft and she was hit by a single torpedo, which jammed her rudder and steering gear. She was now unable to manoeuvre, and the Royal Navy closed in for the kill. Pounded by battleships HMS *Rodney* and HMS *King George V*, and harried by destroyers, *Bismarck* eventually sank at 10.39am on the morning of 27th May 1941. Her end is still a matter of dispute. Did she scuttle herself, as surviving members of her crew claim? Or was she sunk by torpedoes from HMS *Dorsetshire*?

Either way, in the words of Admiral Tovey who had led the hunt against her: "*Bismarck* had put up a most gallant fight against impossible odds, worthy of the old days of the Imperial German Navy, and she went down with her colours flying."

Out of her crew of over 2,200, only 116 sailors survived. HMS *Dorsetshire* had picked up eighty-three sailors (one survivor dying on board the next day) and HMS *Maori*, another twenty-five; but then, the warning went out that there were U-boats in the area and both ships left the scene, abandoning the rest of the crew to the sea. Later on, a German weather ship rescued two more survivors, and the submarine U-74 another three.

THE FIRST GERMAN NAVAL PRISONERS OF WAR in Britain during the Second World War were the crew of the submarine U-27 which was sunk on 20th September 1939. They and others were shipped to Canada in 1940 when a German invasion of Britain was expected. It was not until 1944, after D Day, that large numbers of German prisoners arrived in Britain. In 1939 there had been just two prisoner of war camps in Britain, but by the Allied victory in May 1945, there were 600. It was said that almost a quarter of Britain's

workforce in the immediate post-war years was
made up of prisoner-of-war labour. At first,
supervision was very strict and only good-
conduct prisoners were allowed to work outside

the camps. But gradually conditions relaxed, with families even inviting German prisoners to spend Christmas and other holidays with them.

The first prisoners were sent home in 1946, and by 1949 most had been repatriated; but not all. Out of nearly half a million prisoners, 24,000 elected to stay in Britain. The most famous of these was former Luftwaffe paratrooper Bernhard "Bert" Trautmann. He went on to become goalkeeper for Manchester City, playing in 545 matches for the club between 1949 and 1964. In 2004, Trautmann was awarded an honorary OBE for his promotion through football of Anglo-German understanding.

THE REAL "LITTLE MANFRED" WAS DONATED to the Imperial War Museum by Mr Francis Duke in 2005. During the 1940s, Mr Duke lived with his family on Wested Farm at Crockenhill, near Swanley in Kent, where his father, Fred, was farm secretary. The 600-acre farm employed a large labour force, including German prisoners of war. One of them made the wooden Dachshund dog out of cast-off apple boxes, and also a toy bear, for Francis and his brothers and sister. Mr Duke also donated to the museum a letter written in November 1948 by one of the former German prisoners, Walter Klemenz,

whose home was in the Soviet occupation zone.
In Mr Duke's words, Little Manfred and Walter's
letter both give: "...some insight into how

post-war Britain, or this small part of it, related to its involuntary guest-workers and how, in difficult and abnormal circumstances, they were able to integrate into the community."

Extra Time
by
Michael Foreman

The World Cup
1966

I was there! At Wembley Stadium when England won the World Cup! I had tickets for every England match and many of the other fixtures in the lead up to the Final.

England were not really fancied. The manager, Alf Ramsey, a studious defender in his playing days, favoured hard work and organisation over flair and flamboyance. His England team with their 4-4-2 formation became known as the "Wingless Wonders".

High drama came early. A few weeks before the start of the tournament the World Cup (the Jules Rimet Trophy) itself was stolen

from the "Sporting Stamps" exhibition in Westminster Central Hall. The £30,000 solid gold trophy was stolen but stamps worth £3m were left behind. Brazil, the current holders, said it was a sacrilege that would never have been committed in Brazil, where even its criminals loved football too much to do such a thing. The Trophy was found seven days later, wrapped in newspaper and hidden under a bush in south-east London, by a dog called Pickles.

Group games were spread around grounds up and down the country. The world's best player, Pele, was literally kicked out of the tournament early by tough tackling by Bulgaria in Liverpool. North Korea were the big surprise, sending Italy home early to an airport reception of rotten tomatoes.

England started slowly with a 0-0 draw against Uruguay at Wembley, but then beat Mexico 2-0 and France 2-0 to reach the Quarter Finals. England then beat Argentina 1-0 in a brutal contest. Argentina's captain, Rattin, was sent off. Ramsey didn't allow his players to exchange shirts at the end of the game, labelling the Argentineans 'animals'. England beat Portugal 2-1 in a thrilling Semi-Final and the stage was set for the Final showdown – England v West Germany.

Germany scored first, but Geoff Hurst headed in the equaliser from a free kick by his club mate and England Captain, Bobby Moore. England went ahead in a second half of sunshine and rain, when Martin Peters, the third West Ham player in the team, drove the ball home.

Two minutes to go to the final whistle… I remember the tension, craning forward, waiting for the moment of victory – then the Germans equalised! Extra time… Then the drama of England's next goal – was it over the line or not? The debate continues still.

And then the famous "some people think it's all over… It is NOW!" as Geoff Hurst's thunderous volley completed the victory. Then

the triumphal circuit of the pitch, and the iconic image of fierce-tackling Nobby Stiles jigging about like a schoolboy, holding the trophy aloft.

My mate, Paul Read, was with me at all those games long ago, and he lives to this day on the cliff top at Kessingland. You can see his house in my drawings of Kessingland Beach in this book.

Paul was with me in the huge crowd outside the England team hotel in Knightsbridge, London, on the evening of the victory. Pickles had been invited to the celebrations, and was allowed to lick the plates after the victory banquet.

Pickles licks the Victory plates.

The Jules Rimet trophy

Only 14 inches high, the trophy depicts the winged figure of Nike, the ancient Greek goddess of Victory. During World War II the trophy was held by the 1938 winners, Italy. Ottorino Barassi, the Italian Vice-President of FIFA, secretly removed the trophy from a Rome bank and hid it in a shoebox under his bed to prevent the Nazis from taking it.

Extra Time

In 1970, when Brazil won the Rimet Trophy for the third time, they were allowed to keep it forever. However, in 1983, it was stolen again – in Rio de Janeiro, Brazil! It has never been recovered. So much for Brazil's criminals' great love of the beautiful game...

Michael Foreman

michael morpurgo

A MEDAL FOR LEROY

Illustrated by
Michael Foreman